# The Charnel Caves

Guy N. Smith

SINISTER
HORROR
COMPANY

PRESENTS

# THE CHARNEL CAVES

# GUY N. SMITH

The Charnel Caves

Edited by J. R. Park
Interior design by J. R. Park
Cover design by Vincent Hunt

Published by The Sinister Horror Company

THE CHARNEL CAVES -- 1st ed.
ISBN 978-1-912578-13-9

SinsiterHorrorCompany.com

The Charnel Caves is another installment in the hugely popular Killer Crabs series by Guy N Smith.

Other titles include:

Night Of The Crabs (1976)
Killer Crabs (1978)
The Origin Of The Crabs (1979)
Crabs On The Rampage (1981)
Crab's Moon (1984)
Crabs: The Human Sacrifice (1988)
Killer Crabs The Return (2012)
Crabs Omnibus (2015)

*For Ceri Brown.*
*My sincere thanks for her help and encouragement in the production of*
*my novels over the years.*

1

The young couple strolled hand in hand along the beach leading from Shell Island towards Harlech. Billy Brown, ginger haired with freckled features, had celebrated his twenty-third birthday only the previous week. His girlfriend, Ann Morrison, was eighteen with short dark hair and a petite figure. This was their first holiday together, much to the disapproval of both their parents who still clung to outdated beliefs. Nevertheless, they were camping on the island with just a couple of days to go before their return home to Birmingham.

'It's been a lovely week,' she stretched up to kiss him, 'even if it has been too hot to do anything more than just lie in the shade. Yesterday, I'm told, it was thirty degrees. Phew! Thank goodness it's cooled off a bit this evening. By the way, Billy, I was chatting to somebody in the shop who said that forty years or so ago this coastline had been invaded by crabs as big as cows. I don't believe it.'

'Well, my dad told me the same. He was on holiday with Mum and, according to him, dozens of these monsters came up out of the sea. Everybody had to run for it. He said the army was called in and there was one helluva battle. But you know how stories get exaggerated over the years. There must be some truth in it though.'

'Well, I just hope we don't meet up with any,' she squeezed his hand. 'It'll be dark soon, so don't you think we had better be heading back to camp.'

'There's no hurry,' he replied. 'You're not getting jittery, are you?'

'Hold on!' She stopped suddenly, peered into the gathering dusk. 'What's that's up there, sprawled over that rock?'

He stared up ahead of them. Even at their distance in the encroaching gloom there was no mistaking a human body, a female with arms and legs splayed, a torn dress revealing much of her naked body.

'Stay here!' Billy's outstretched arm prevented Ann from following him as he advanced with faltering steps. His mouth was dry, he was trembling.

He halted a yard or so from the girl, noted the array of deep wounds on her breasts and stomach, like she had been lashed with a whip, pale blue incisions which appeared to curl over the top half of her body. There was no doubt that she was dead, killed by something beyond his comprehension.

'Billy, what's going on?'

'Don't come any closer. This… this girl died in… a

very strange way. Like... like she's been...whipped to death. I'll... I'll phone the police... we'll have to stay around until they arrive.'

'Oh God!' She thought she was going to vomit.

With shaking hands Billy made the 999 call. He had to convince the police operator that it wasn't a hoax. Finally, he pocketed his mobile and walked back to join Ann.

'They're on their way.' He turned and stared out to sea, unable to bear looking upon that inexplicable horror any longer.

Ten minutes later a police Land Rover arrived on the road up above followed by an ambulance. A coastguard vehicle brought up the rear.

The body was loaded into the ambulance. Two police officers remained in discussion with a coastguard. Only then did they approach Billy and Ann.

'We'll need a statement from you,' an officer addressed them. 'I think you had better come to the station with us.'

'What killed the girl?' Billy blurted out.

'We won't know for sure until there has been a full investigation and autopsy,' the officer was non-committal.

Detective Chief Inspector Williams had been called

out, a tall, taciturn man with thinning grey hair. He was less than a year off retirement and it was obvious that he could have done without this latest problem.

'Well, I'd better take a statement from you two,' he produced a pad from his desk, motioning Billy and Ann to sit down.

'The dead girl is believed to be the daughter of Mr and Mrs Elton who are spending a week's holiday in Llanbedr. Our officers have gone to break the sad news to them and ask them to identify the body. I...'

He was interrupted by a tap on the door.

'Come in!' A terse command.

The newcomer was of slight build with thinning hair. 'I got your call, inspector,' he spoke with a distinct northern accent.

'Ah Professor,' Williams looked up. 'I'm sorry to disturb you from whatever you were doing but I would appreciate you knowing the events of this evening. Obviously, we shall not know the cause of death until a full autopsy has been completed, probably by tomorrow.'

The newcomer grimaced.

'This is professor Danielson of the Marine Conservation Society,' the inspector nodded to the couple seated opposite him. 'I would like you to tell him how you first saw the dead girl.'

Falteringly Billy described their initial discovery of the corpse. He felt nauseous, Ann was pale and trembling.

'At this early stage I am convinced that she was the

4

victim of a Lion's Mane Jellyfish,' Danielson stated. 'They are becoming increasingly common in British waters, mostly due to climate change. There have been sightings off Walney Island in Cumbria and three swimmers were injured, but fortunately survived in Galway. There are several species, but the big one can attain a size of 120 feet long. The largest blue whale has a length of 108 feet!'

Billy pursed his lips and paled.

'Warmer seas increase plankton levels,' Danielson continued. 'These creatures use their tentacles to catch and eat fish and other marine creatures including smaller jellyfish. Doubtless this girl was killed by one although it had not got around to devouring her. Perhaps human flesh is not to its taste!' He gave a humourless laugh. 'Anyway, it is obvious that there is a danger to bathers and swimmers in these coastal waters. Obviously, we cannot ban holidaymakers from them, but I think it is imperative that warning notices should be displayed at intervals long the beaches.'

'I agree with you,' Williams nodded. 'I will contact the council tomorrow to see what they can arrange.'

'I'll leave it to you then.'

'Now,' the officer stood up, 'I think we've about finished here. Mister Brown, I shall doubtless be needing to speak to you again before you leave the Welsh coast. With luck we shall have a report confirming the exact means whereby Miss Elton died. I shall dispatch one of our lady officials to comfort the parents in these tragic circumstances. Professor, I suggest we meet up in the morning, say around eleven o'clock and determine our next move. Thank you all for your co-operation.'

He sighed aloud. He had an uneasy premonition that the horrors were only just beginning.

2

Guy N. Smith

Cliff Davenport stared in horror at the scene before him on the seafront at Barmouth. His mouth was dry, sweat tricked down his lean features. Giant crabs the size of cows were clawing their way up the sea wall, a dozen or so with more following them out of the incoming tide.

An army platoon had arrived, the air was filled with the sound of gunfire along with the clicking of monstrous claws. A couple of bathers had attempted to flee but were pulled down, limbs torn from their bodies, blood spouting.

An RAF helicopter hovered above, more gunfire but the bullets ricocheted off the huge shells. The leading crabs made it ashore, people were fleeing, parents clutching young children to them as they ran. An elderly man stumbled and fell, becoming the first land victim of the attackers. The clicking of pincers was akin to gunfire answering that of the military defenders.

Davenport wanted to flee with the rest of the holidaymakers, but his legs refused to move. Now one of the crabs had singled him out and advanced towards him.

'Cliff... Cliff. Wake up. You're having one of your nightmares again!'

Hands were shaking him, frantically attempting to bring him back to reality. He thrust the damp bedclothes to one side, kicked them free of his sweat soaked body, stared up into the attractive features of his wife.

'Oh, thank God!' Sheer relief flooded over him as he sank back on the pillow. Just another nightmare. They had been recurring all too frequently since those terrible days of the crustacean attacks on Barmouth and Shell Island all of forty years ago. Would they never cease and leave him assured of a peaceful night's sleep?

'That was a bad one,' Pat Davenport slid off the bed and straightened her nightdress. 'Try to relax, Cliff, whilst I go downstairs and make a cup of tea.'

This latest nightmare had been the worst of all, so real just like he had been back there in person witnessing the carnage. He was still shaking. Then an idea filtered in to his somewhat confused brain. He would discuss it with Pat. A successful career as a marine biologist and all forms of undersea life was escalating to a terrifying climax in his retirement.

Numerous visits to a psychiatrist had done nothing for him. Now he had the germ of an idea for a new approach. Anything was worth trying. Soldiers returning from the horrors of war suffered similar phobias.

'Here you are love,' Pat placed a hot mug of strong tea on the bedside table and lowered herself into a chair. 'That really was a bad one, it was almost impossible to shake you awake.'

'Yes,' he sipped his drink. 'A very bad one. Psychiatrists are a waste of time, but I've had an idea, it came to me just after you woke me.'

'Go on.'

'Well, I think a holiday would do us both good.'

'I'd love it. We haven't been away anywhere since you retired. Abroad maybe?'

'No,' he averted his gaze. 'I was thinking more of… Barmouth.'

'Oh Christ!' Her expression was one of shocked surprise. 'No way, not there. You have frequent nightmares about the place, and it would really bring it all back to you. And me. I never want to see that place again for as long as I live.'

'It'd be different now, all peace and quiet.'

'But the memories would still be there, for both of us.'

'I'm thinking that for us to stay there, see it as a typical Welsh holiday resort, it might wipe away the horror of the crabs.'

'And what about that article in the paper last week, a young girl found killed on the beach by a giant jellyfish? Is that why you want to go back there, Cliff? Hunt some other kind of horrible sea monster?'

'Not at all', he smiled. 'I know about them, nothing I could do to help. But I might have a word with

11

Professor Danielson at the Marine Conservation Society if he hasn't retired yet. I worked with him on a couple of occasions in the past. It would be good to meet up again.'

'Couldn't we go and stay somewhere else, maybe Brighton or Bournemouth, well away from the past?'

'I think Barmouth might help my crab phobia. Seeing it as it is now might wipe those memories away.'

'Maybe,' she pursed her lips. 'But I'd want to book in somewhere completely different. That B&B in Wellington Terrace was great, but it would have reminders for both of us. I suggest a hotel somewhere in the town.'

'That's fine by me,' there was no mistaking the relief in his smile. 'Anyways, I heard that Richard Lloyd is dead, and I doubt that Ruth would have kept the place going on her own. I'll book us in at a hotel.'

'And preferably one without a sea view,' she wagged a finger at him.

They both laughed.

3

Guy N. Smith

'Good to see you again, Cliff,' Professor Danielson was slight of build and balding. Cliff had rarely seen him smile, a man devoted to his job and doubtless regretting his forthcoming retirement. 'The modern generation have no recollection of that crab invasion, just heard a few stories which most of them dismiss as rubbish and that can only be good. Now, though, as you probably know we have a problem with these giant jellyfish moving in to UK waters. There has been a human victim.'

'So I've heard.'

'I could use somebody with your experience of marine life.'

'That's not why I'm here. I don't want to get involved with any more creatures coming ashore and attacking folks. If I can satisfy my troubled mind that the monster crabs no longer exist then hopefully I will be able to sleep at night without having horrific nightmares.'

'Fair enough.' A rare smile. 'Carry on, Cliff. But there are a few changes taking place on Shell Island. Hopefully the former emergency system will be able to continue.' He explained in detail the proposed emergency procedures. 'So have a walk around the beach, satisfy your troubled mind that the crabs have gone forever.'

'Thanks.' Davenport turned towards the door. 'I'll keep in touch and pray to God I don't have anything to report.'

Dawn was now breaking when Cliff eased himself out of bed and began to dress.

'I wish you weren't going to walk up the coastline,' Pat stirred.

'I'm sure it's absolutely safe,' he shrugged his jacket on, picked up the ornamental stick which he always used, not that he needed it. It had been carved for him as a Christmas gift by a stick making colleague, the handle a lifelike pheasant's head. 'You catch up on some sleep. I'll be back in time for breakfast.'

'I sincerely hope so.' She knew only too well that she would not sleep until her husband returned safely. This coastline had some terrible reminders of years ago.

The beach and the view across to Shell Island looked

exactly the same as they had all those years ago. Davenport stood there taking in the scene. Holiday makers on the Island were up and about. He could not repress a shudder as memories came flooding back. No, apart from a few giant jellyfish there in the sea there was nothing to worry about, he convinced himself. All the same, he was a little uneasy.

The tide had already turned exposing areas of the shoreline, wet sand that glistened in the early morning sunlight. A couple of small crabs scuttled amongst the rocks. Cliff grimaced at the sight of them. Even though they were of the common variety they had him tensing, they were reminders of their giant relatives.

'But the monsters are gone,' he spoke aloud just to reassure himself. 'Gone, gone for good!'

There was a line of litter left by the tide, waste plastic of all kinds. He grimaced at the sight. Maybe a team of local volunteers would be down later, on a clean-up operation as was happening in many other coastal areas.

He came to the foot of the cliffs, towering rocks that had withstood a battering by the waves since time immemorial. His route took him beneath them. Shortly he would turn back, breakfast was calling him.

The walk had had its benefits, though. He felt more relaxed within himself having viewed this seascape which had once held unbelievable horrors. Tomorrow he would walk in the opposite direction, hopefully before the storm which was forecast arrived. The so called weather experts were already issuing red warnings, changing from amber. They reckoned that it would be one of the worst to hit Britain in many years. Well, he and Pat would sit it out in their holiday accommodation.

Just as he was about to retrace his steps, he noticed some strange markings on the sand amidst the beach pebbles, a mass of lengthy flails like somebody had wielded a multi thronged whip, washed by the receding tide but still just visible.

'Strange!' He pursed his lips and bent down to examine the markings closer. That was when realisation dawned on him. Giant jellyfish! Like the one that had killed that young girl recently. A pang of fear had him glancing around but there was nothing in sight except those two small crabs and a tiny jellyfish. No way could the latter have made those marks.

Then he saw the cave at the foot of the cliff, a wide opening at beach level that was filled with water which had not followed the tide out. A kind of miniature lagoon which stretched into the rockface, probably never drained. Mostly it would go unnoticed or be disregarded by holiday makers.

Then he stiffened as his searching gaze picked out some other marks amidst the stony surface; huge gouges which had scraped some of the pebbles aside. A few of the smaller ones had cracked beneath the pressure of a heavy weight pressing down on them. The marks led from that cave and there were others that returned to it.

In that brief moment Cliff Davenport's phobias, his worst fears, returned. There was no doubt in his mind that those deep ruts had been made by the pincers of giant crabs. All the evidence pointed to the return to these shores of those monster crustaceans of yesteryear.

He straightened up, instinctively backed away and glanced all around. There was no sign of any form of life except seagulls wheeling overhead and those two small crabs moving out to the receding tideline.

'I don't believe it!' Again, he voiced his fear aloud. A shiver ran up his spine.

Undoubtedly the monsters had been in that flooded cave, so its interior had to be fairly extensive, probably going far into the base of the cliff, and permanently flooded by the sea, maybe a kind of underground lagoon. There had been no reports of sightings, so it seemed that they were lying low here. Biding their time. Planning another attack on mankind?

There was nothing he could do right now. The purpose of his visit to the scene of carnage some four decades ago was already proving to be disastrous. No way would his phobias be dispelled in the light of that which he had discovered this morning.

He started on the return journey to Barmouth. Breakfast first and then he would make a call upon Danielson.

'Well,' Pat regarded him across the table, 'how did your early morning walk go?'

'An invigorating breath of sea air and some welcome

exercise,' he avoided her searching gaze.

'You seem somewhat troubled, Cliff,' she fixed her eyes on him, sensing that something was amiss. 'Too many memories coming back? I said at the outset that it was a mistake to return here. You seemed somewhat shaken when you got back from your ramble.'

'I shall be fine,' he snapped. 'I didn't expect everything to be fine and dandy at the outset. Now, if you can amuse yourself this morning I want to make a call upon Professor Danielson.'

'Which means you've seen something out there.'

'Just signs that those giant jellyfish have come ashore on the incoming tide. Notices warning bathers of their presence in these waters have already been erected.'

'Then there's nothing much to discuss with Danielson. Cliff, please don't get involved in another invasion by marine monsters. There's nothing you can do.'

'Except give him the benefit of my knowledge of marine life after a career in studying it.'

'Oh, well, I suppose there's no harm in that, but I wish that we hadn't returned here. The idea was to cure your phobias.'

'That's what I'm working on,' he snapped, pushed back his chair and rose from the table.

'Well, I didn't expect to see you again so soon,' Professor Danielson rose from behind his desk. 'I take it you've been on an early morning exploration of the beach.'

'Yes,' Cliff lowered himself into the chair opposite, 'and I'm rather concerned by what I discovered.'

'Oh?' The other raised his eyebrows. 'Jellyfish, I presume.'

'They're around, but I have reason to believe that those giant crabs are back on the Welsh coastline.'

'Never! Impossible!'

'There's a flooded cave at the base of the cliffs up towards Harlech. There are undoubted signs that the crabs are using it, an ideal hideout for them… until they are ready to attack again!'

'Nonsense. I know the cave you mean, it's permanently flooded and how far it goes beneath the cliffs I've no idea. Only fully equipped divers would be able to penetrate it.'

'Well, there are signs that the crabs are using it, doubtless lying low by day and emerging to hunt for food after dark.'

'If I wasn't aware of your reputation as a marine biologist I would laugh,' Danielson sank back in his chair, 'but I'll take your word for it. The problem is what are we going to do about it. I will discuss it with the coastguards, and we shall need to examine the exterior of the cave, look at the tracks you mention. Then, if we are convinced, we'll arrange for a diver to investigate.'

'That's a very dangerous proposition.' Cliff's lips

tightened.

'There's an excellent marine diver in the vicinity, a young man named Adrian Thomas. He takes underwater photographs, some of which he sells to magazines. A few weeks ago, there was one of his of a monster jellyfish in a national newspaper, He's our man if we need him.'

'I'll leave it to you.'

'As you know, changes are taking place on Shell Island. It is now owned by Llanbedr Airfield who purchased it in 2012. Snowdonia Aerospace proposes that it will become the site of the UK Spaceport, a centre for the testing and development of drone technology. However, the safety of their staff and holidaymakers must be a priority so the Welsh Government is being petitioned to reinstate guaranteed high tide emergency service access. If the crabs really have returned, then there is likely to be unimaginable danger both to holiday makers and the technology installed there. We need to find out what, if anything, is going on in those caves as soon as possible.'

'All right, I'll work with you in an advisory capacity,' Cliff nodded. 'But if the crabs really have returned then I'll be away from here like a shot.'

4

Guy N. Smith

Adrian Thomas had been deep-sea diving since his mid-teens. Now, in his 28th year, he was fresh faced and virtually always wore a permanent smile. He was well liked in the Barmouth area where he worked as a motor mechanic.

The influx of giant jellyfish was somewhat concerning but already they had done him several favours with his photographic hobby. The picture of that monster which he had sold to a daily paper was a huge bonus. They had paid him more than he earned in a week at the garage. He was determined to photograph another, they were really in the news after that girl's death.

'I wish you'd find another hobby,' Amy his attractive partner sighed as she watched him sorting out his diving apparatus one morning. 'I can never relax when I know you're down there in the deep.'

'There's good money in it,' he kissed her.

'One or two more pics like that last one and we'll be able to put a deposit down on a house, get married and have kids.'

She smiled. His promise did not lessen the risks but it was a nice thought.

'Where are you going today then, love?'

'Martin's going deep sea fishing so I'll go with him.'

'Well, at least you'll have company, somebody to summon help if you need it.'

'I'll be fine,' he kissed her again and went outside.

Martin Rees was in his mid-forties, had fished all his life, relied mostly on those who travelled to Llanbedr for his services. He had an annual list of regular clients, enough to earn him a modest living.

Squat of build with a weather-beaten face, he had never married, lived alone in a small cottage. One of his regulars, Frank Walters from the Midlands, was booked in for next week. Frank paid well so today he could afford to take Adrian out with him. It was a big responsibility having somebody down there in the deep, but the guy was experienced.

Anyway, Martin was glad of the company.

'I want to find another of those huge *jellies*,' Adrian announced as he clambered aboard Frank's 20ft boat.

'Maybe bigger than the last one, and close up.'

'You be bloody careful,' Martin grunted as he cast off. 'You know what happened to that poor lass. What will I do if one of the buggers gets you?'

'Call the coastguard,' Adrian laughed.

'A lot of bloody good that'll do. So just watch out, I don't want the bastards up here. They'd sink my boat.'

'Just keep that big knife of yours handy,' Adrian laughed. 'Chop their bloody tentacles off!'

They lapsed into silence. Adrian began donning his diving gear and checked the underwater camera. Always an optimist he had the feeling that this was going to be his Big Day.

'Wish me luck.' He gave a parting wave to his companion as he lowered himself over the side of the boat and into the water. Diving down he was once again in a magical world, one which never ceased to excite him; so many species of ocean life all around. He took a few photos, most of which he had on his records anyway.

Then he saw the huge jellyfish resembling an upturned bell with a mass of tentacles spilling down from it about fifty metres away. This one was even larger than that previous sighting which he had photographed and sent to the press. It was drifting to and fro obviously searching for small prey.

Adrian was cautious but not afraid as he moved in closer, camera at the ready. Now he had an unrestricted view of those tentacles which appeared to be in three or four rows. Like broad arms. A mass of them clustered around what was obviously its mouth. He estimated that the trailing ones were around 30 metres or more in length.

The creature had singled out a cluster of shrimps. Its tentacles moved with amazing speed, closing over its prey. Another photograph, then Adrian was aware that the mighty predator had noted his presence and was turning towards him. It was time to leave.

As he struck upwards, he noted something else some distance from himself, a huge shape crouched on the sea bed amidst a cluster of rocks. However, its shape did not conform with those jagged stones, too smooth and rounded. It moved, part of it lifted in what he interpreted as a kind of threatening gesture.

Just a brief view as he glanced behind him and saw his mighty pursuer coming closer. His priority was to reach the fishing boat above and clamber to safety.

One final look down. The water was murky but there was no mistaking that second occupant on the sea bed. It was a crab of immense size, now crawling out of its resting place. Oh, Jesus! There was now sheer panic in his upward flight to safety.

After what seemed an eternity, he reached the fishing boat above, scrambled over the side at any second expecting one of those long tentacles to encircle him and drag him back into the water.

'Whatever's the matter?' Martin reached out to assist him.

'Jellyfish,' Adrian grunted as he tore his head free of his headpiece. 'Right behind...'

At that moment a mass of tentacles slithered over the side of the boat, the creature's sheer weight below threatening to capsize the craft.

Martin grabbed a heavy, sharp bladed knife from the tray of equipment which he used for gutting any large specimen of fish his client might catch. He swung it above his head, bought it down on the gripping mass of dark purple wriggling, clinging horrors from the deep.

'Grab a knife,' he shouted. 'I can't keep up with these!'

Adrian scrambled in the box, found another heavy bladed gutting tool, then joined his companion in slashing and dismembering. As they cut through the gripping tentacles more and more slithered up out of the threshing sea.

The boat rocked from side to side, threatening to capsize, a variety of equipment slithering across the deck.

'Keep slashing!' Martin yelled.

Severed tentacles floated on the water prior to sinking. Then much to both men's relief the fishing boat stopped rocking.

'Phew!' Adrian leaned against the side, exhausted. 'I won't go as far as to say we've killed the bastard but at least it's released its grip. Let's hope it's gone back down to suck its wounds.'

'I reckon we'd better head back to shore as quickly as possible,' Martin wiped his sweating brow.

'There's… there's something else down there,' Adrian's voice trembled.

'What?'

'A… a crab… as big as a bloody cow!'

'Jesus Christ! I don't believe it!'

'Well, I saw it! No mistaking it!'

'So, they're back, after forty years. We'd better let the coastguards know.'

'I'll speak to Professor Danielson at the Marine Conservation Society. I made his acquaintance after I photographed that giant jellyfish which appeared in the paper. Then it's up to him. Right now, I'm not doing any more diving after what I found down there!'

Right now, all both men wanted was to be back safe on dry land.

5

Guy N. Smith

The Russian submarine had crept low into the English Channel, slowly edging its way up into Welsh waters; the most up-to-date model manufactured by the Soviets so far. With a hull length of 70 meters it weighed 3076 tonnes, was fitted with six torpedo launch tubes and was capable of carrying a 205-kilogram explosive charge. It could also release 24 mines and eight anti-aircraft missiles could be fitted. Its crew were afforded an endurance of 45 days when submerged.

Its fittings also included the very latest technology designed to render it undetectable from both the surface and the air, invisible to both patrolling helicopters and warships which might be patrolling above in search of any violation of their waters. The electric engine emitted less heat, a vital factor in it not being detected.

In effect this was a test run to establish invisibility to all kinds of technology used by defence patrols. Both warships and submarines had been escorted out of

British waters in recent times. Hopefully this one would prove its invulnerability to any patrols above the ocean surface. It carried neither missiles nor weaponry of any kind, its sole object was marine invisibility to those who might seek to detect its presence.

There was a crew of just three, all high ranking GRU officers, Alexander Boshirov was in command, dark haired and bearded, a permanent stoic expression which rarely betrayed his innermost thoughts. His two subordinates were secretly in dread of him, such was his power both on land and below the ocean.

Vladimir Vladimirovich was lean and clean shaven, his attention constantly fixed upon the array of technical apparatus before him. Anatolly Petrov was a heavyweight by comparison with the other two, florid features and deep sunken eyes. All three had been awarded medals for past services by Vladimir Putin himself and were regarded as highly suitable for any important missions to be undertaken. As was this explorative underwater venture into British waters.

'So far so good,' Boshirov broke the long silence and there was a hint of both relief and satisfaction in his tone. 'The latest system which is designed to reject any highly technical means of detecting our presence by our enemies is proving successful. Neither aerial nor surface patrols have picked us up across the British channel. Not that,' he gave a rare smirk, 'they have a sizeable number of craft for the purpose. Just two seaborne Border Force vessels which are failing to cope within a seven-thousand-mile coastline. Its other two vessels are deployed in the Mediterranean and Aegean because of the European migrant crisis. Further to that,' he gave a faint snigger, 'their latest warship, a 65,000-ton aircraft carrier, has gone to the USA. Britain is highly vulnerable to any activity by our country as we have already proved.'

'How far into Welsh waters are we going?' Petrov enquired somewhat hesitantly for their chief did not welcome input from his subordinates. They were his servants, here to obey and not query his instructions.

'Very soon we will begin our return journey,' he replied. 'I will instruct you accordingly.'

That was when they heard a faint scraping on the exterior of the craft. It increased to a loud screeching as though something was tearing at the heavy armour-plated hull.

'You have made contact with a heavy sharp rock!' There was anger in the chief's tone. He turned back towards a rear port hole. The submarine was impregnable but any exterior damage however slight, would bring the wrath of their GRU superior down upon them.

Water and marine growth were foaming over the porthole; it was difficult to determine what was causing the ear-splitting screech of tortured armour plated steel.

The other two followed in his wake, staring, attempting to identify whatever it was amidst the swirling water. A brief moment of clarity revealed a huge claw frantically ripping at the exterior.

'Whatever is it?' Vladimirovich gasped, relieved that

he had not scraped their vessel against a protruding sharp rock.

'A… claw of some kind!' Petrov grunted, 'Whatever it is, is trying to gain entry!'

Boshirov's face was pushed up against the porthole. Now he had a partial vision of a huge creature with a massive shell covering its body and a pair of tiny eyes which glinted malevolently.

'What on the manner our mother country!' Boshirov's tone embodied both disbelief and fear. 'It's…it's a huge crab, the size of a horse!'

All three recoiled instinctively, disbelief and terror at that which they saw crouched on the seabed, a claw raised for another strike.

'Move on!' Boshirov shouted. 'Move away, quick!'

The other two rushed to obey, trembling hands fingering the engine controls.

There was no response. It was as though the entire mechanism was dead.

'It's wrecked the systems somehow,' there was panic in Petrov's voice. 'The submarine is grounded!'

'Impossible!'

'Try it yourself!' He would not have spoken to his commander in that tone in any other situation.

Boshirov pushed his companion aside, crouched over the controls. The engine screen was black, he could not bring it back to life. An eerie silence except for the ear-splitting screech made by their attacker.

'No way can it get into us,' Boshirov voiced his hope. 'Nothing can.'

'But we're stuck at the bottom of the Mawddach Estuary!' Vladimirovich groaned. 'We can't go anywhere!'

'Then we have to call Moscow for help. They will have to contact the British authorities to dispatch a rescue. It could be worse, just a political row over our trespass in these waters. It has happened before.'

'Contact them. At once!' There was now rare panic in Boshirov's tone.

'How.. how long will it take to get help to us?' There was no mistaking the fear in Petrov's reply.

'In theory we can survive up to forty-five days in here. That's always supposing that the in-built atmospheric meter works throughout. But, of course, we don't have sufficient supplies of food and drinking water. This was only supposed to be a trial mission to discover whether or not we could sneak in and out without being detected by British patrols.'

Petrov turned back to the array of instruments. The starting mechanism was still dead; he had not expected it to reinstate itself. He moved on to the communications section, pressed a button. Once. Twice. There was no response.

It was as dead as the other instruments

The three occupants of the submarine stared at one another in dismay.

'We're stranded!' Boshirov voiced their worst fears. 'We can't start the motors and we have no way of summoning help. Somehow that crab has wrecked our only lifelines!'

A silence except for the continued battering of that mighty crustacean claw at their rear.

Then came another sound, a steady drip… drip.

'What's that?' All three of them stumbled their way back to the rear, fearful of that which they might see.

They stood in horror at the scene which greeted them. The sizeable porthole, reputedly strong enough to withstand anything against which it might come into contact, had a crack from top to bottom through which a steady trickle of seawater flowed.

'It's cracked the glass!' Petrov shouted aloud. 'We're all going to drown.'

Outside the giant crab continued to hammer with its huge claw.

6

Guy N. Smith

'You're surely not going back out there tonight!' Pat Davenport stared aghast across the hotel dinner table at her husband.

'I need to take a look by night, darling,' Cliff tried to speak reassuringly. 'After all, there's a full moon and there will be ample vision. Rest assured, I shall not be taking any risks, just a look up and down the shoreline to see if anything is about.'

'Like what?'

'I've no idea until I see something.' He had considered it wise not to mention those crabs' marks to her. After all, he could not be absolutely certain that the giant crustaceans had not returned to their 40-year-old territory. He just needed to satisfy himself.... from a distance. Unless he went back on a look-around he would never know for sure. In all probability he would not see anything at all.

'Well, I won't be able to sleep until you are safely back here,' she stated in a sulky tone and poured herself a second cup of coffee.

It should have been a magical night down there on the shoreline where the tide had receded and would shortly be turning. A full moon shone brightly, and a myriad of stars glittered in the cloudless sky. Yet for Cliff Davenport it was a sinister scene, bringing back too many memories of those distant years. Could it be that the monster crustaceans had really returned? Those claw scrapes up by the cliffs indicated that they had. He shivered. No, surely not.

He passed along by Shell Island. There was still plenty of activity from the camping site, fires burning, holiday makers cooking late suppers on barbeques. Children laughed and shrieked. Everything seemed so normal, just as it should have been. Apart from the litter, mostly plastic waste, which had not blighted the scene in the old days.

Up ahead the cliffs towered. Almost there. He would take a quick look around, see if there were any visible signs of... well, anything on the stony tide-washed beach.

Notices were displayed at intervals, recently erected to warn bathers of the presence of giant jellyfish. The authorities had not wasted any time in putting them up.

He approached the flooded cave with caution. As he had expected the entrance resembled a sizeable pool that never drained. It was dark and foreboding.

Out on the litter strewn tideline something moved.

He stared, tensed. A huge shape with elongated tentacles struggling to free itself from a mass of plastic bags and other similar waste.

It was a huge jellyfish that had become caught up. Briefly he pitied the creature, hoped that it would manage to free itself. No marine life deserved such a fate.

Then he came upon some of those gigantic scrapes amidst the tide-washed stony beach, huge gouges heading seawards and then returning towards that dark pool. He used his torch to examine them at close quarters. They were three- or four-feet long indentations and a shiver ran up and down his spine. There was no doubt in his mind what had made them, a huge crab! Just a single crustacean.

It had emerged from that sunken cave, headed seaward and then returned to its hidden refuge at the foot of the cliffs. In all probability it had emerged after darkness had fallen, gone on a hunt for food and then returned.

There was no doubt in Cliff's mind and the sooner he returned to the safety of the hotel the better. Tomorrow morning, he would call on Professor Danielson, try and convince him that there was at least one giant crab living in that flooded cave. How far the cave extended beneath the cliff was another matter. There could be a network of them, a hideout for a number of crabs. Danielson had informed him that as far as he knew nobody had ever explored the interior of the base of the cliffs. A deadly secret could well lurk in there; a threat to the holidaymakers in the area. If so, then action of some kind was needed sooner rather than later.

He found himself hurrying on the return walk, instinctively glancing behind him every so often. All was relatively quiet on Shell Island; the majority of campers having retired for the night.

'Well?' Pat was still fully dressed, sitting in the small lounge of the hotel. There was no mistaking the expression of sheer relief on her face when he entered.

'I just don't know', he decided that a non-committal answer was the best course at this time of night. 'I guess I'll have another chat with Danielson in the morning. The only sign of life I saw out there was one of those damned jelly fish caught up in a heap of plastic waste. Poor bugger!'

'Like yourself, I really don't know what to think,' Professor Danielson was seated behind his desk and there was no mistaking the concern on his face. 'We don't have anything concrete to go on but one thing's for certain, those caves have to be explored by a competent sea diver and the only one I know locally is a guy name Adrian Thomas. He's recently been in the national press with some stunning photos he took of jellyfish deep down in the bay.'

'It would be a very dangerous exploration,' Cliff's expression was grim. 'In the light of what I've seen there's at least one crab in there. There could be more.'

'Agreed, but somebody will have to go in. We'll have the coastguards in attendance also on the entrance just in case. I'll give Adrian a ring; test his reaction.'

He picked up the phone, dialled a number. A woman's voice answered.

'Oh, I see, well thank you. I'll call again.'

'He's away today', he replaced the receiver. 'I'll ring him this evening and see if we can arrange something. In the meantime, I'll have a word with the coastguard. I rather think, Cliff, that at this stage nobody's going to believe us. We need concrete evidence before anything positive will take place. Strange, on his last diving exploration Adrian told me he thought he saw a big crab in the distance on the sea bed. I must admit I took it with a pinch of salt, you can't always be sure of what you see down there in the murky depths but what you've told me casts a different light on the matter. First, though, I need to talk to Adrian. Then we'll go from there.'

Guy N. Smith

7

Guy N. Smith

Frank Walters had farmed a small acreage in the Midlands all his life, taking over the land after his father's death around ten years ago and managing it up until his recent retirement, growing an annual crop of potatoes, carrots and other vegetables. Six mornings every week he had made a trip to Birmingham market to deliver fresh produce, all very tiring and boring.

Now he had sold the land and was enjoying a peaceful retirement in their small cottage on the edge of a hamlet with the wife, Fran. For the first time in their married life they took three or four short holidays every year, two of which were sea fishing trips to the Welsh coast.

Frank's weather-beaten features spoke of a life outdoors, greying hair and powerful shoulders. A keen gardener he kept his half acre immaculate and grew most of their own produce.

'Well, everywhere's nice and tidy and Bill will check the greenhouse daily,' he swilled his hands in the kitchen sink, 'so we can be off nice and early in the morning.'

'I've already packed,' Fran placed two steaming plates on the table. 'I'm really looking forward to a week away. I've just heard the weather forecast, there's one of those tornados moving across from the east coast of the states but with luck it won't be hitting the UK until later in the week so hopefully you'll be able to get a couple of hours fishing trips in before it arrives. By the way, Martin Rees phoned earlier just to confirm that he's all set to take you out fishing the day after tomorrow.'

'Excellent,' Frank lowered himself into the vacant chair. 'Fingers crossed we'll enjoy the best of this weather whilst it lasts and come home with a few mackerel.'

Martin Rees had had second thoughts about another fishing trip after that episode with the giant jellyfish when he had taken Adrian Thomas out with him. Phew! That had been a scary experience, the pair of them chopping the creature's tentacles off as it attempted to climb aboard. They had been mighty close to capsizing.

Yet he was in no position to abandon his livelihood, he was a few years off retirement yet. He relied upon paying fishermen and supplying two or three shops in the area. It was just bad luck, it probably would not happen again. Just as a precaution he sorted out two really heavy knives and razor sharpened them in readiness. I'll really cut up the next bugger, if there is one, he reminded himself! All the same he had to get used to going out to sea.

Why the hell didn't the coastguards make some effort to cull the bastards? Because in this stupid day and age conservation was uppermost in the minds of the public.

'Good to see you, Frank.' Martin's confidence had returned by the time his client arrived the following morning. 'Weather looks good, ideal for our trip.' He indicated the moored 20ft fishing boat. 'I've got plenty of bait, worms, small crabs, slices of mackerel so we're well prepared. Let's get aboard and see what we can do.'

About half a mile from shore Martin dropped anchor and handed his companion a baited line. 'We'll give it half an hour here and see how we get on. If there's nothing doing we'll move a little further on towards Harlech.'

All seemed unusually quiet; their lines remained slack.

'I'd've thought we'd've had a bite by now.' Rees had a puzzled expression on his rugged features. 'I've never known it so quiet, just like every fish around here has buggered off.'

His thoughts returned to that jellyfish. Maybe the buggers had been hunting in the vicinity and all marine life had scarpered. He glanced towards the array of heavy knives which he had placed in readiness for an emergency. He was tense, worried also that he might have brought his client out on a blank day.

'We'll find 'em.' He moved to restart the engine and that was when something struck the bottom of the craft, a shuddering blow, rocking it from side to side.

'What the fuck!' It was no jellyfish, no slithering tentacles creeping over the side to secure a grip. Somewhat unsteadily he rose and peered down into the water.

'What the hell's going on?' Frank grabbed for a hold and was almost unseated.

'Jesus Christ!' Martin could scarcely believe what he saw, a gigantic crustacean reaching up from the rocky bottom and waving a huge pincer. Woodwork cracked, the hull began to split, water gushing into the small craft.

'It's one of those bloody gigantic crabs! It's smashing the boat to get at us!'

Fishing rods were dropped as the occupants of the boat sprawled headlong.

'The boat's sinking. Swim for the shore!'

Both men splashed into the water, sank, surfaced. Swimming was virtually impossible with their heavy waders impeding them.

The creature turned its attention away from the damaged boat, seeing human prey within easy reach. Pincers wavered, then struck with unerring aim and force. An instant amputation of the Welshman's right leg. A snap at the left, the water around the injured fisherman swirled and turned scarlet.

Frank wallowed, it was a struggle to keep his head above the surface. Panicking, threshing and then the huge crab was upon him, slashing and tearing, a maelstrom of crustacean fury.

Bleeding limbs sank, surfaced, drifted. A severed head with trailing flesh, an unexpected feast gifted to this devil from the deep.

To the rear of the carnage the damaged fishing boat slowly sank, disappearing from view.

Unhurriedly the crab fed and then shambled on in the direction of the towering cliffs.

Hidden from view it would await the coming of darkness before returning to its lair. It had long learned how to outwit humans.

Dusk was already deepening, and Fran was becoming increasingly concerned when there was no sign of her husband. She was expecting him back by their traditional five o'clock teatime.

Maybe he and Rees were having a bumper day, a couple of baskets filled with mackerel and still catching them. She attempted to console herself with this thought but, with still no sound of footsteps on the narrow path leading up to their holiday accommodation, she decided to take a walk down to the quayside. If they had not already landed, then she might well be able to see them out in the bay.

She found herself hurrying. The sun had already set out in the west and darkness was closing in. In all probability she would not be able to spot them out there.

They're surely okay, she kept telling herself. Frank was that type of bloke, he was always fine in any situation.

The quay was deserted. A couple of fishing boats were moored there, their occupants probably back in their homes sitting down to a well-earned meal.

But where the hell was Frank and Martin?

With a shaking finger she dialled her husband's mobile. There was no response, it was unobtainable. It might be due to atmospherics, she tried to console herself, there were mountains all-around the coast.

She was starting to panic and that was when she heard footsteps approaching. Oh, please let it be Rees and Frank. It wasn't, instead a courting couple heading down towards the beach.

'Oh, please,' she blurted out as they approached her. 'I can't find my husband. He went fishing with Martin Rees…'

The tall youth cast a glance across the harbour, then shaded his eyes and scanned the darkening bay. 'No sign of his boat,' he muttered, 'and that's strange. He's usually back long before dark.'

'Where can he be?' There was a note of desperation in her voice. 'My husband's gone on a fishing trip with him. He said they would be back by late afternoon.'

'Could be they've popped to Harlech. Can't say for sure.'

'There's something wrong,' Fran wrung her hands together. 'I know there is.'

'Tell you what,' the youth produced his mobile. 'I'll call the coastguard at Barmouth, see if they can shed any light on it.'

'Oh, thank you.'

The other made the promised call which was answered almost immediately. He explained, a brief conversation followed.

'They're putting a boat out right now. They'll do a tour of the bay. You couldn't have better help. Rest assured, if Rees is in trouble with his boat, engine failure or whatever, they'll tow him back here.'

The coast guard boat arrived within twenty minutes, manned by a crew of two, eased up to the jetty and helped Fran aboard.

'Don't you worry, love,' a tall man wearing a woollen hat, smiled reassuringly. 'We're always getting routine call-outs like this, rarely anything serious. We'll circle and then check Harlech. We'll find 'em for sure.'

The craft chugged out steadily, embarking upon a wide sweep of the bay. There were no other boats in sight, most of the local fishermen and pleasure cruisers had packed up for the day.

'Well, they aren't stuck out here,' the coastguard

scanned the bay with his binoculars. 'I guess we'll take a quick look at the boats moored at Harlech and then head back. Bet you we find 'em back at Llanbedr.'

'I sincerely hope so.'

'Hey, just a second,' the coastguard at the controls called out. 'There's something over there, can't make out what it is. I'll move in closer.'

The three of them strained their eyes, peering through the gathering dusk. Something floated on the surface, bobbed on the incoming tide, disappeared then showed itself again.

'What the bloody hell is it, Steve? It looks like some sort of dead marine life.'

'Move in closer,' the other produced a long rake which had been lying on the deck. 'I'll fish it out so we can have a look. It's probably nothing to concern us but we'd better check.'

It wasn't easy to secure the bobbing object. It almost seemed that it had a life of its own and was determined not to be caught. He swore beneath his breath but finally, with a swift downward and upward sweep he caught it in the prongs of his rake, lifting it, dripping, clear of the water.

As he hauled it aboard, he saw it clearly in the reflection from the pilot's light. He stared in horror and disbelief at the object which was now impaled on the prongs of the rusted rake.

'Jesus Christ!' He recoiled, giving a cry of revulsion as it hung down. It was a human arm, a mass of bloody shreds dripping where it had been torn from the shoulder of a corpse.

Stubby fingers moved as though they still had life left in them. And on the third finger a gold wedding ring glittered.

'That's Frank's arm!' Fran let out a hysterical scream, clutching the side of the boat. 'That's his wedding ring!'

The dismembered limb fell to the deck with a resounding squelch, forefinger extended like it was pointing back to the sea where it had been retrieved; a warning even in death that further horrors lurked below.

'There's wreckage floating over there,' the man at the controls could only manage a hoarse whisper, 'and… and something else!'

He refrained from glancing behind him where his companion was supporting their distraught passenger. He did not want to view whatever bobbed amidst what was obviously the wreckage of the fishing boat for which they had been searching. He steeled himself; it was his job.

'Hand me that rake, Joe.'

With no small amount of difficulty, the pilot began probing amidst bobbing wreckage.

Damn it, where was whatever he had glimpsed. It had sunk. It resurfaced, it was like a small football in shape, a mass of seaweed draped over it as though it was attempting to screen him from yet another horror from the deep.

He caught it and with no small amount of difficulty, raised it clear of the water. From the tangled weed which covered it, two dead eyes stared up at him. The object in question was a human head above a ragged mass of flesh from the bloody neck and throat, the mouth wide open like it was still screaming, even in death.

It thudded to the deck, rolled, came to a halt, seemingly staring up at those who had retrieved it from a watery grave.

'What is it, Ewan?'

'It... It's a human head. I... I recognise it... it's been ripped from... Martin Rees's body. God, whatever did this, sank the fishing boat and then ripped the two of them to ribbons!'

'A giant crab,' Ewan whispered, afraid to voice his suspicion aloud. 'Remember, Adrian Thomas thought he saw one down here when he was photographing jellyfish. Can't be anything else.'

'We'd better radio for help, get this poor lady ashore. The monster that did this has got to be found and destroyed before there's another attack. And the sooner we're away from here, the safer I'll feel!'

8

'I told you it was a mistake coming back here,' Pat Davenport shook her head and stared at her breakfast plate. The last thing she felt like was eating. They had come back here to try and cure her husband's phobias and now it was as though they had resurrected the past.

'I had a walk down to the sea front earlier,' she added. 'My God, it's like nothing has changed over the past forty years. There was a platoon of armed soldiers and a gunboat scouring the bay. I heard that a couple of fishermen have been horribly killed by a crab, or crabs. There's talk that those monsters have returned Cliff... I think the best thing we could do would be to return home and let them sort their own problems out here.'

'In which case my nightmares and phobias will only continue. Probably get worse.'

'If that's possible.'

'If the crabs are lurking down there then they've got

to be located and wiped out before there's another inshore invasion.'

'But you can't do anything, Cliff!'

'Professor Danielson has asked me to assist in an advisory role. Don't forget, my career has been studying marine life.'

She sighed.

'I've arranged a meeting with Danielson this morning. I'm convinced that there are crabs here, not a huge army of them like there were before, but just a few and they're using flooded caves beneath the cliffs.'

'You're not going to go down in there, are you?' There was a hint of panic in her voice.

'Don't worry, I'm not. I'm too old for those kinds of capers these days. As I said my role will be solely in an advisory capacity. Nobody knows how far those caves go into the cliffs, how big they are, but the main drawback is that they are permanently flooded. I have no doubt in my mind that that is where these crabs will be located, a virtually impenetrable hideout. If that's the case, then exterminating them is going to be far from easy. Armed soldiers won't be able to operate in there. Rest assured, Pat, I shall not be going in there.'

'Well, that's a relief,' she picked up her knife and fork. 'I guess then that I have no option but to go along with whatever you have in mind.'

'And at this stage I have no idea,' he smiled reassuringly. 'First, we have to wait and see what the armed forces find on the sea bed. If anything!'

Cliff stared in shocked amazement at the scene which greeted him on the seafront at Barmouth and stretching out towards Shell Island. Milling crowds of sightseers were jostling one another whilst police were attempting to keep them off the beach.

Out at sea, two naval gunboats moved in a widening circle whilst overhead a helicopter hovered. Some huge and heavy task was being undertaken on the tideline, heavy machinery dragging a submarine out of the water assisted by cranes.

He trembled slightly, it was akin to turning back the clock to those days when the military were raking invading crustacean attackers with heavy mortar fire.

Except that there were no crabs in sight. Thank God! So, what the hell was happening?

He hurried back towards the HQ of the Marine Conservation Society and tapped on the door of Danielson's office.

On entering he was somewhat surprised to find a group of half-a-dozen military officers around the desk, a large-scale map spread between them.

'Come and join us, Cliff.' The Professor's expression was grave. Clearly there had been some dramatic happenings in the hours after daylight.

Cliff leaned up against the window, all the chairs were taken. More reminders of those distant days flooded his mind, Colonel Goode and Commander Grisedale amongst several other top personnel. They had long retired; were probably dead. This was the modern equivalent of those top military men. In all probability they had only heard rumours of those terrible days. Clearly though, something dramatic had already happened.

'Much has been happening over the last few hours,' the senior military officer took over the meeting, he was clearly bemused and troubled by recent events. 'Due to a horrendous attack on a fishing boat late yesterday, the coast guard called us. According to the mutilation of the fishermen it has all the signs of a giant crustacean attack. Hence helicopters with underwater technology have been scouring the bay and a warship was drafted in as an additional precaution. No crabs but as the tide ebbed, they spotted a damaged submarine on the sea bed!'

Davenport's jaw dropped. This whole business was getting beyond belief.

'Heavy tack was summoned,' Colonel Sanderson stroked his clipped moustache. 'It was dragged ashore. Russian, of course, but somehow it had eluded our regular patrols with the latest technology which should have revealed any such craft sneaking into UK waters. It had obviously moved up from the English Channel undetected.'

'Strewth!' Davenport was stunned. The others glanced at one another clearly as bemused as he was.

'It had been attacked on the seabed,' Sanderson continued, 'and the initial exterior damage had

64

succeeded in allowing water to trickle inside. The three occupants had drowned and clearly their very sophisticated system which would have enabled them to call for assistance had been put out of action. The exterior damage, as far as we can ascertain at this stage, had been inflicted by a huge crab which had attacked it!'

A shocked silence descended upon the gathering. Davenport clutched the windowsill behind him. He was trembling.

'The submarine in question,' Sanderson continued, 'is of the latest Russian designs and can be used for TEST-71 MKE TV Electric -homing torpedoes and can carry a 205-kilogram explosive charge as well as releasing 24 mines. It is also fitted to accommodate up to eight anti-aircraft missiles. It can dive up to 300 meters below the surface. It is something of a relief to find that it was not carrying any warfare equipment. It would appear at this stage that it was primarily a reconnaissance craft, fitted with the latest technology to render it invisible to our patrolling ships and helicopters. Its presence in UK waters would have gone unnoticed – except for this attack, presumably by monster crabs!'

'Unbelievable!' Davenport voiced his innermost thoughts and fears. 'But, as you say, Colonel, there are no signs of crabs lurking out in the bay. What about the crew?'

'By now their bodies should be on their way to Porton Down where their cause of death will be identified. I have no doubt in my mind that it was simply by drowning, trapped in a damaged sub and unable to summon help. They are, we believe, high-ranking Russian GRU agents but that remains to be established. Then undoubtedly our government will contact the Kremlin and demand an explanation. Not that that will amount to much other than to add to the growing tension of the new Cold War!'

'So,' Davenport's voice had a slight tremor in it, 'we know that the crabs have returned to the Welsh Coast but they are lying low.'

'Professor Danielson informs us that you have already made some investigations, and, in your opinion, they are hiding out in some hidden flooded caves beneath the cliffs. Is that right?'

'I have little to go on except crustacean marks in the region of the cave entrance, Colonel.'

'Then we should be grateful for your help. You have had a lifetime's experience in marine life as well as having been involved in the crab attacks here some forty years ago.'

'I would be more than willing to help,' Davenport nodded and added, 'but only in an advisory capacity. No way would I consider exploring those caves myself.'

'Of course not, I fully understand. We will arrange that. However, we must ensure the safety of holiday makers without creating alarm and panic. Armed soldiers will be on hand… just in case!'

'According to the news there's a hurricane moving towards the UK which will not help the current situation. I suggest that we go and examine the beach below the cliffs and perhaps formulate a plan of action.'

'I've managed to contact Adrian Thomas,' Danielson announced as the gathering rose to their feet, 'and he will accompany us. Needless to say, that Russian sub dragged up on the beach is attracting the attention of hundreds of holiday makers so let's treat it as an accident and announce that it must have struck a hard object on the sea bed. We don't want the press featuring a crab's story on their front pages. Our priority is to discover where the crabs are hiding and destroy them as unobtrusively as possible.'

Guy N. Smith

9

Guy N. Smith

Ioan Hughes had lived in a remote cottage on the outskirts of Harlech all his life. Now aged 40 his parents were dead, and he continued a hermit -like existence making a sparse living out of doing odd jobs for neighbours and fishing. He had always had a fear of boats and, unlike Rees Jones and several others, he never fished from one. He relied upon the shoreline and whatever the tide bought in, mostly shrimp and crabs.

His squat features sported a mass of blackheads, and his short but powerful figure shuffled rather than walked. He was a standing joke for the local school children who teased him from a distance. He rarely washed, never bathed, and a strong body odour followed his wake wherever he went. Whenever he visited the local small shop the proprietor sprayed deodorant after his departure.

That said, he was hard working and honest.

He had checked the latest weather report. the big storm was on the way, it would probably arrive in a couple of days which meant that shrimps would be following the incoming tide, seeking safety closer to shore. It was an unprecedented opportunity for a sizeable catch.

It was late afternoon when he set off for the shoreline carrying a couple of plastic buckets and his fishing net. The stretch below the cliffs was always a prime area for scooping up sizeable catches. With luck he would fill both buckets within the hour. Then he would return home, pick up some fish and chips, maybe a pizza, from the small shop en route. That done, he would sit out the forthcoming hurricane and return on the following day to see what it had washed up. Plastic litter was always a nuisance, it added to the difficulty of scooping the tideline and he had to extricate all manner of rubbish from his net before tipping out his catches.

God, it was humid today, a sure forerunner of the impending hurricane. Ioan seated himself on a convenient rock and took his time rolling a cigarette. There was no immediate hurry. He regarded that sizeable pool which he had never known empty. He wondered idly to where that cave led, probably a long way inside the cliff. Doubtless it filled from further up inside and was always topped up by the tide.

Now, time to start work. Plagued by old childhood fears he did not like being out and about on the beach once darkness fell. He recalled the stories his folks had told him about the giant crabs that had invaded the coastline. He had been a baby then, too young to recall any of the happenings. They were probably grossly exaggerated, at least he almost convinced himself that they were. He preferred not to think about them.

Now those giant jellyfish had moved into the bay. He had not seen one himself but there were warning notices all along the coastline. Still, if he kept to the tide's edge, he was unlikely to come upon one.

It was a long time since he had seen hordes of shrimps such as were in evidence along the tideline. He scooped his net, the cane handle bowing, threatening to snap. Bloody rubbish, he scooped out all the kinds of litter, cast it aside and drained wriggling shrimp into his bucket. He would be finished earlier than anticipated, then stagger home with his catches.

It was then that he detected a kind of clicking sound somewhere to his rear. He ignored it; it was probably smaller pebbles being washed down into that pool.

Scooping, discarding rubbish, tipping squiggling shrimps into the second bucket. He was sweating heavily; his BO was very strong.

More clicking, much louder this time. He glanced behind and gave a strangled scream at the sight which greeted him, the half-filled bucket falling from his grasp.

There, no more than a few yards away, a huge crab crouched on the edge of that rock pool, a pincer raised and a small face with tiny eyes regarding him. The size of a small pony, there was no mistaking its intent. It had emerged in search of available marine life food and was confronted with human flesh for the taking.

Ioan froze, a strangled scream in his throat. He made to flee, stumbling clumsily on the stony beach, caught his foot on a small protruding rock and fell headlong. Struggling to rise it was as though his body had undergone a sudden paralysis. His foot was trapped amidst some pebbles, his shaking arms were incapable of lifting his body upright.

Click-Click-Click. The Giant crustacean advanced, scraping its mighty pincers on the rocks. One was lifted threateningly; a sweeping movement and it closed over Ioan's outstretched leg, dragged it free, pulled him towards it. Evil eyes bored into his own. He felt that pincer gripping him, cutting into flesh and bone.

'No!' He managed a piercing scream.

The crab could easily have ripped his body apart and fed upon the exposed flesh which was already bleeding profusely. Instead though, it began to drag him back towards the pool from which it had emerged. A mighty splash and he was submerged, drowning, his arms flailing limply. Sharp splinters of rock embedded themselves in his skull, then came blessed oblivion.

Sometime later dusk merged into darkness and the only sound on that stretch of beach was the lapping of the incoming tide.

It was the following morning when the party arrived on

that stretch of beach below the towering cliff face. Cliff had had a lift in the military vehicle accompanied by Sanderson and a couple of armed soldiers. The Coastguard Land Rover had followed with two coastguards accompanied by Professor Danielson and Adrian Thomas. The tide was receding as they made their way along the stony beach.

Sanderson had already been contacted by a scientist at Porton Down. The trio from the submarine had died from drowning, there was no other cause of death. Undoubtedly, they were Russian GRU senior officers and it was up to Whitehall to establish their identification and the reason for their presence in UK waters. Not that there would be any useful information forthcoming. The Kremlin would doubtless request the return of their corpses.

In all probability that would be agreed but only after their true identities had been established.

As for the damage to the submarine, experts had already agreed that it had been inflicted by huge sharp claws which had belonged to a massive creature, possibly a crustacean.

'And now we have another missing local,' Sanderson informed his companions. 'It was reported by a neighbour who had gone to his cottage to purchase some shrimps, knowing that this man, Ioan Hughes, had been fishing on the shoreline late yesterday. I... just a minute, what's that on the edge of the tide?'

One of the soldiers slopped his way through the shallows to retrieve it.

'It's a plastic bucket,' he held it aloft, 'and there's some dead shrimps in the bottom.'

'Doubtless having belong to Hughes,' Sanderson took the bucket, shook his head. 'Well if he had had some success, he certainly didn't take his catch home with him!'

Davenport examined the stony ground below the cliff face. Unfortunately, the tide had removed any tracks which otherwise might have been visible.

'What's that on the rocks above the pool?' Adrian was peering closely at whatever had attracted his attention. 'Looks to me like splashes of blood which the tide hasn't reached and they've dried off!'

Cliff Davenport strode ahead of his colleagues, peering closely where the other had indicated. He pursed his lips and an icy shiver ran up his spine.

'It's blood, all right,' he announced in faltering tones. 'And at a guess I'd say it has come from a human being. I may be wrong...' he hoped fervently that he was.

'There's more there,' Adrian pointed to the top of the flooded cave. 'Like whatever was responsible dragged its victim through this pool and into the cave!'

There was a stunned silence amidst the gathering. Maybe they had guessed what the caves hid from human view but now they were faced with stark proof. Crabs. Just a simple monster or several?

'Well?' Sanderson was the first to speak. 'What do we do now? Where do we go from here?'

All eyes focused on Adrian. He knew only too well what was going through their minds.

Somebody had to go in there!

'It might not be accessible,' he was clearly in awe of the prospect of venturing inside the cave.

'If a huge crab can get in there then the cave, or caves, have to be pretty sizeable,' Danielson stated.

'There might be a jellyfish in there,' Adrian replied. 'You saw for yourself what they did to that poor girl. They can reach an awful long way with their tentacles. If they get hold of you then you don't stand a chance. As for crabs I can swim faster than they can shamble.'

'There won't be jellyfish in the caves,' Cliff spoke as reassuringly as was possible. 'What I know of those monsters, and I had plenty of experiences years ago, the jellyfish wouldn't stand a chance. They would be ideal crab food, take it from me.'

'Well,' Sanderson was seeking a positive answer, 'are you prepared to give it a go or not? If not, then I shall have to find some deep-sea divers from somewhere. Time is not on our side and according to the weather forecast a hurricane is due to hit this part of the coast very soon.'

'All right, I'll give it a go,' Adrian nodded. 'Tomorrow morning. I'll need to get kitted out.'

'Tomorrow morning, ten o'clock, no later,' there was no mistaking the other's relief.

'And what if there are crabs in there,' Danielson voiced the thoughts of the others, 'how do we deal with them?'

'I'll have armed military on standby. We may have to blow up the cave entrance, trap them in there with no means of escape. All I'm asking you to do is to establish their presence there. We'll see to the rest.'

The party made their way back to the parked vehicles.

'I'd like you to accompany us, Davenport,' Sanderson placed a hand on the other's shoulder; 'You don't have to do anything except stand by. We might be glad of your knowledge and experience. I don't envisage any risk. After all, we've got 'em trapped in there. All we need is confirmation by this young man that there are crabs lurking in those caves. We'll set up an explosive device in readiness and once he emerges with positive information that will be it. No risk to anybody!'

# 10

Guy N. Smith

'Oh, please don't go with them,' Pat Davenport wrung her hands together. 'You've done your bit, established that crabs are using those caves. Why can't you just leave it to the others to deal with them?'

'I won't be taking any risks, I promise you,' he replied. 'I shall just be a spectator, available to give any advice necessary. In all probability the crab, or crabs, won't emerge. They'll keep to their hiding place and once Adrian is back safely the military will blow up the cave entrance and trap them in there. As for myself, their final destruction will help to destroy all those damned phobias that I've had over the years.'

'Well I guess I can't stop you,' she shook her head in resignation. 'I shall sit here worrying myself to death the whole time you're away.'

Emotional blackmail. He shrugged off a sense of guilt. This time the entire crabs saga would be put to bed once and for all. It was important to think positively.

The Military Land Rover picked him up from the hotel shortly after nine o'clock. He squeezed into the rear seat alongside Danielson and Adrian Thomas. The latter was fully kitted out in his underwater diving suit. He nodded to Cliff but did not speak. There was no mistaking his tension. He had hardly slept during the previous night.

Down on the shore the party gathered. Once again Cliff inspected the pebbled beach in front of the cave. If that creature had emerged during the nocturnal hours, then the tide had removed any tracks it might have left. In all probability it had feasted on its human prey and had had no need to search for food outside.

The soldiers set up an explosive device close to the cave entrance and just above the water level. That done they looked to Sanderson for further instructions.

'Well, I guess we're all set,' their commander stated. 'How about you, Thomas, are you ready to go?'

'I guess so,' the other gripped his headpiece. 'Hopefully I'll be back soon.'

'Shine your light in every corner, and if you so much as see one of those crabs get the hell out of there as fast as you can. All we need to know is that the cave is being occupied by them.'

Adrian nodded and lowered himself into the pool. It was waist deep at the entrance merging into a narrow channel which disappeared below the cliff face. He ducked under the entrance, shining his beam inside.

From here on it was akin to a wide stream, dark

foreboding water up to his waist. The beam lit up the area beyond and he noted that the channel veered to his right, then disappeared round a sharp bend. Ahead of him, on his right, a rocky shelf above the water level. He hauled himself up on to it, here it was easier than wading through the channel.

There was another bend some fifteen meters ahead of him. He wondered just how far it penetrated the cliffs. There was only one way to find out...

Outside on the beach the small party had clustered into a group, all eyes focused on that pool. Nobody spoke; there was nothing left to say.

The breeze had stiffened, overhead the sky was clouding. A few spots of rain were a forewarning of the mighty storm which was out there crossing the Atlantic Ocean.

Everybody prayed that before long Adrian Thomas would emerge safe and sound. If he had found any evidence that giant crabs were holed up in there, then this business could be bought to a swift conclusion. The soldiers would detonate that explosive device and then that would be that.

The rocky tunnel divided into two, one going straight ahead, the other veering off to the right. Adrian's beam only allowed him to see around ten yards ahead of each. Clearly both twisted and turned, shaped by a natural water flow from up above over many thousands of years.

The ledge on which he walked splashed beneath his feet, but it was still navigable without swimming in the main channel which widened and then narrowed in places. It was a kind of underground river, now more than just a stream.

Right or left? If he had had a coin to hand he would probably have taken a decision on heads or tails. He decided to continue to his left. He could always return and explore the other.

After ten yards or so this rocky tunnel became higher and wider. The depth of water on the ledge beneath his feet was no more than a foot or so. The going became easier. Christ how much further before…

Two diversions to the right and left. It was as if separate water flowed from higher up and converged here. He chose the left-hand route, it was a winding one, much wider than the others, a rocky ledge high above the watercourse below.

Another tunnel led off to the right, but he ignored it. This place reminded him of a gigantic rabbit warren. He knew that he had to keep a mental note of all the turns if he was to find his way back to the entrance.

It was drier here beneath his feet, probably due to the

increased elevation. That was when his powerful beam picked up something in front of him, a stain that stood out starkly from the dark rock. He bent down to examine it closely.

God Almighty! There was no mistaking what it was… a blood stain. He recalled those scarlet splashes on the rocky entrance which Cliff Davenport said had come from a human being. Ioan's disappearance, the fisherman was believed to have been taken by a giant crab, the corpse dragged back to wherever the monster, or monsters, hid from human presence.

Until they were ready… for what?

Adrian hesitated; he was trembling. Maybe he should go back now whilst he was still safe, tell the others what he had discovered. Yet it was not definite proof, not enough to blast the rocky entrance. That way they would never know for sure. The crab or crabs might be out in the ocean hunting for food.

He had to continue, a little further at least. Then if he did not come upon definite proof that this awful place was inhabited by monster crabs, he would call it a day.

Jesus, it was awful in here, Nature's own catacombs!

Again, the passageway divided, a narrow stream to the left, a much wider one to his right. He decided to follow the latter.

More blood stains. If the creature was carrying Ioan then the latter was bleeding heavily.

Something else stood out on the dark ledge up ahead. He hesitated, focused his beam on it.

A human leg, torn away from its body just above the

knee. Ripped flesh trailed from it in gruesome strands!

*Turn back whilst you still can!*

It was as though a voice inside him was issuing a frantic warning. Just one more bend up ahead. He would take a look around it and then make his departure. Surely, he had seen enough already.

Somewhat hesitantly, fearfully, he crept around the ledge which veered off to his right.

Then suddenly he found himself standing on the perimeter of a mighty cavern, maybe thirty feet high and even wider, its base a large and deep underground lake.

There was a massive rocky shelf on the opposite end with the water lapping at its edges. A kind of island with the channel much narrower and flowing down from beyond it on both sides.

Yet it was this unusual 'island' which bought a gasp of horror from him. Crouched there amidst a virtual jungle of marine growth a pair of massive crabs regarded him with wicked tiny eyes which reflected his torch beam. Around these were a group of much smaller crustaceans, their sizes varying from those of a large dog down to domestic cat proportions.

Even Adrian's shocked brain recognised the purpose for which these underground caves were being used. Doubtless the huge creatures were a breeding pair which were in the process of rearing a revolting nursery of their own kind, hidden away from mankind until they had enough to launch an attack, continuing where their ancestors had been annihilated four decades ago. Mankind's most dreaded foe had returned to their former haunt!

Adrian was trembling in every limb, his legs threatening to crumple from underneath him on that rocky ledge. He gave a stifled scream of terror, deafening within his waterproof headgear. Already the larger of the two parent crabs was easing its way into the underground lake, its evil twin orbs fixed unwaveringly upon yet another feast of human flesh.

Somehow, he forced his shaking body to move and made an unsteady turn to his rear. He almost fell but somehow regained his balance. Flight was the only option to him, back the way he had come.

Christ, he hoped he could remember all the twists and turns. One factor in his favour was that once he was back on the narrow ledge the crabs could only pursue him in the water. He would be within its reach but maybe he could travel faster than his pursuer.

Please God, I hope I can make it make it back to the beach!

He heard the crab splashing in the water, its mighty pincers scraping on the rock.

Certainly, it was hampered by its narrow surroundings. Don't try to run, you'll fall, he kept telling himself, and don't look behind. Just keep going.

A turn to the right where the caves and watercourses temporarily parted. They would join up again further on and then it was a left turn for Adrian. He prayed that his memory served him correctly.

Down below, just a few yards behind, his pursuer was scraping its way through the channel. Thank God the ledge was too narrow for it to clamber up. A massive pincer was uplifted but it could only scrape the edge of the elevation.

For a moment he lost sight of it as he entered the left-hand passageway. After that he would emerge back onto the ledge. One final turn and he would come to the big pool at the exterior. He would need to hurry then in case his pursuer caught up with him. Once he was out of the caves the military would doubtless put paid to that crab and blow it to smithereens.

Back on the ledge, his beam picked out another passageway. It had to be the one he was seeking although the entrance seemed much narrower than he recalled. Still, he told himself, one's surroundings were likely to seem somewhat different in this murky darkness.

He had to squeeze through. Behind him that crab was rattling a pincer on the edge of the ledge. It was clearly angry and frustrated by the disappearance of its intended human prey for which it hungered.

Adrian groped his way along the rocky passage. It had not been so narrow on his previous exploratory mission. Even narrower still; something was definitely wrong.

Then, suddenly, that tunnel ended, just a rock face that denied him any further progress.

He fought down rising panic. There were so many caves leading from this narrow ledge, he must have passed this one without noticing it. Maybe the one he sought was further down.

No big deal, he told himself. All he had to do was to retrace his steps, continue along the rock shelf until…

As he turned, his beam picked out a mighty pincer clawing a hold on the ledge, reaching up with another, lifting it threateningly.

There was no way the crab could climb up onto that raised track, there was not room enough for its huge body. Yet that claw could reach up and across blocking his exit. There was no way Adrian could continue his flight.

He was trapped within that narrow opening, crouched at its extremity, transfixed by that claw poised to rip him to shreds if he approached within reach of it.

It had already tasted human flesh and now it hungered for more.

Guy N. Smith

11

'Where the hell's that boy got to?' Sanderson glanced at his watch; it was now past mid-day. 'Something's gone wrong. I'll see if I can get hold of Wilson, a diver who has helped us out in the past when we've been looking for drowned migrants trying to cross from Calais. As it happens, he only lives at Dolgellau. I wish I'd contacted him before we began this business!'

He reached out his mobile. The incoming tide was now strengthening, waves dashing against the cliff face. The small gathering moved further down; they were already soaking wet up to their waists. Dark clouds were moving in, bringing increasing heavy rain with them. The hurricane was approaching sooner than had been forecast.

'We're in luck.' Sanderson pocketed his phone. 'Wilson was at home. He's heading out here right away, but he'll have one helluva job coping in this storm.'

They huddled, waited, there was nothing else they could do. Even the two soldiers had retreated to a rock pile which afforded sparse shelter.

Nobody spoke. There was nothing to say. Clearly Adrian was in trouble of some sort.

An hour later a 4-wheel drive mini pulled up on the cliff road above. Calvin Wilson had arrived.

'He's somewhere in there,' Sanderson had to shout to make himself heard as the other donned his diving gear. 'And for God's sake don't you get lost too!'

Wilson was small and lithe with a close clipped beard, an experienced diver since youth.

'I'll do the best I can,' he promised, 'but it looks real bad and will only get worse as the waves increase. If I can't see any sign of this guy, then I'm packing it in. Diving in open water is one thing, in there is highly dangerous. I'll give it half an hour, no more.'

'All right. Best of luck.' Sanderson watched the other make his way towards that pool which was already starting to overflow. The diver disappeared and the long wait below the cliff face began.

Cliff Davenport considered returning to the hotel in Barmouth to put Pat's mind at rest.

He regretted not having come here in his own car for no way were his companions going to pack up yet. Certainly not until one or both divers emerged safely. If there was no sign of Adrian, then surely they would not detonate an explosion and risk trapping him in there along with whatever else might inhabit those caves.

The final decision was up to Sanderson.

'All we can do now is wait,' Sanderson and the others had grouped behind some jutting rocks fifty yards or so down from the entrance to the cave. The two soldiers had joined them, leaving their explosive device by the overflowing pool. The wind was gathering force, the heavy rain horizontal. 'The Terror from the West' as the media called it would be at full force early in the coming evening.

'It will be interesting to hear how the Russians explain the presence of what appears to be their latest and most technically advanced submarine in UK waters.' Cliff smiled wryly.

'Doubtless Putin will come up with the usual lies, blame the British, claim we wrecked it.'

'I've no doubt the Foreign Office have already contacted them,' Sanderson replied 'and we'll hear something ridiculous shortly. The corpses will have to be returned but I've no doubt that sub will be remaining in Britain until every aspect of its technology has been unravelled. That way our armed forces and coastal patrols will know exactly what we are up against. The Cold War can only intensify. I guess the crabs have done us a big favour, If they had not attacked the sub then it would have sneaked back to Russia and our authorities would have been none the wiser. Nevertheless, if that cave is the crustacean's secret refuge, we have to destroy them. It will be interesting to know, if possible, how many of them are in there.'

'I reckon there's more than one,' Cliff shook his head, 'but we'll only know when your diver returns. Hopefully he will also locate Adrian. I'm somewhat concerned that he hasn't shown up, he's been in there three hours already.'

Adrian cowered at the rear of the small, narrow recess. He removed his face mask; he did not need it to breathe although the air was somewhat stifling. Otherwise he would surely have suffocated by now.

The crab was still in the channel below. It had given up scraping with its pincers, there was no way it would climb up on to the narrow ledge with its mighty, cumbersome body.

It sank back into the channel with a mighty splash, its huge shell scraping against both sides. One claw rested against the ledge, held in readiness in case the trapped human should make a break for freedom. It was in no hurry. Adrian crouched at the extremity of that small opening in the rock face. He felt sick and physically weak. He considered making a rush for freedom on the off chance that he could avoid that pincer, scramble his way out to the exit which could only be a matter of thirty yards or so beyond the next bend. He might or might not be successful in his bid for freedom; if only his legs were not so weak he might have stood a slim chance. Moving around down here strained every muscle in the body.

All the time water was rushing down the channel below, he could hear the waves crashing against the cliff face beyond. He switched off his lamp, there was no point in wasting the battery. Now he cowered in total darkness. It was terrifying and he knew that he had to make a decision soon. He could either stay where he was and suffer a lingering death or make a rush for freedom and probably be ripped apart by a giant claw.

Calvin Wilson waded through the swirling pool, the water up to his chest. The beam from his light showed him where that ledge jutted above the surface. With no small amount of difficulty he pulled himself up on to it and found that there was room enough for him to stand upright with the top of his helmet scraping against the rocky roof.

The surface was uneven and in places small fallen rocks were a problem in keeping his balance. Up ahead the tunnel veered off to his right. His powerful beam showed him a wall and roof which dipped into water.

Not a nice place, he told himself. He much preferred

diving into the open sea where he could see all around him with ample warning of any danger. Here it was claustrophobic with nowhere to flee if the need arose.

The channel widened and as his beam swept the surface he saw the huge crab crouched there, a monster which had no right to exist. A claw was wedged on the brink of a ledge a couple of yards from another narrow tunnel.

Its eyes glinted in the dazzling beam. It did not move. Its attention had been focused on the narrow opening and beyond its reach.

Those evil orbs turned to focus on him. Surprise and indecision. Its crustacean brain was momentarily confused.

That was when Calvin detected a faint human cry from within the opening ahead of him, indecipherable but undoubtedly a strangled plea for help. It could only have come from the missing diver held at bay by this terrible creature.

'Adrian?' Calvin's voice echoed down the tunnel, 'Adrian… Adrian…'

'Help me.' This time the voice from that recess was unmistakable; a desperate reply which embodied both relief and sheer terror.

'Stay where you are Adrian!' If the other emerged he would doubtless be seized by a pincer which opened in anticipation. Christ, what do I do now? Calvin froze, his beam fixed on the crab's small face. Its eyes glinting greedily. He sensed that momentarily it was as surprised and confused as himself. He had to take advantage of its brief indecision; a brace of human prey, which one should it attack first?

Lost for choice it hesitated.

Calvin directed the powerful beam of his lamp directly on those evil orbs. They glowed brightly like coals in a fire about to burst into flame. The creature halted, bemused, the pincer dropping down from the ledge above where it had been scraping.

'Adrian!' Calvin's shout echoed down the passage beyond. 'Get out now, head this way as fast as you can!'

There was a moment or two of silence and then Adrian came stumbling from the small cave, clutching at the rocky sides of the ledge for support, using his own beam to guide him.

He had no idea who his attempted rescuer was, but another human was sheer relief.

'Head this way. Follow me!' Calvin's beam had certainly disorientated the crab but for how long? It wallowed and splashed in the deepening channel.

'Carry on towards the exit, I'll try to confuse the bastard as long as I can.'

Adrian stumbled, almost lost his balance and fell but somehow remained upright.

Progress was difficult on the uneven surface and both men knew that when they reached the flooded pool they would need to go underwater, fight their way against the increasing, raging current until they emerged into the open. If they made it that far.

Calvin backed away, following the other, trying to keep his balance and avoid plunging over the edge. If that happened, he would be easy prey for the crustacean.

Still dazzled, the crab's fury at this sudden disturbance was only too clear. Pincers waved from side to side, disturbing loose stone which splashed down into the water. Human prey was here for the taking, it was determined to catch one or both of the men.

'Keep going!' Calvin yelled to the other.

Although dazzled and confused the crustacean was using its pincers to aid it in its pursuit, scraping the rocky sides of the fast-flowing water course as the only guide it had to the pursued. Its shambling gait was fast reducing the distance between them.

Adrian lowered himself in to the current, fighting against it, as it threatened to sweep him back along with Calvin who was close behind, pushing at him.

Now they clutched at each other for support. God, how much further? Additional turmoil was being caused by those gigantic claws which powered the beast in their wake.

Then both divers were clear of the passage beneath the cliff face, pulling themselves up on the rocky beach, but it was imperative to maintain their flight until they reached safety.

Some distance away they were just able to make out a group of men attempting to shelter behind a pile of rocks, waves crashing against it. They waved; their shouts lost in the tearing gale. The small rescue group of military and coast guards had been reluctant to desert their divers although they had almost given up hope of seeing them again.

Yet the danger was far from over. The pursuing monster emerged from the cave entrance and crouched on the rocks. Shots rang out from armed soldiers. Bullets ricocheted off the giant shell, but the monster appeared to be impervious to gunfire.

Calvin and Adrian wallowed in the rushing incoming tide, and were almost battered against the cliff face. A glance behind showed the crab had ceased its pursuit as a mighty foaming wave struck it. It halted, watching its prey disappearing and then turned back the way it had come. It was not prepared to risk venturing into the open raging tide.

'It's going back into the cave!' Calvin's cry of relief was whipped away by the tearing gale. 'Keep going, we'll make it yet!'

Soon they had joined the waiting group huddled behind the pile of rocks which afforded scant but welcome shelter.

'Thank God you're both safe!' Sanderson shouted in sheer undisguised relief.

'There's crabs in there all right,' Adrian's voice shook as he recalled what he had seen. 'Big 'uns and little 'uns, and stinking dead 'uns. It's a breeding hideout until they're ready to launch a full-scale attack!'

'Blow the cave up. Bury them alive!' Sanderson addressed the two soldiers.

'No chance,' came the reply from a saturated uniformed sergeant. 'We'd never get back to the cave now and even if we did, I doubt that our explosive equipment would still be there on the rock where we left it.'

Sanderson nodded his reluctant acceptance. 'I guess you're right. Well, at least everybody's safe and we know that the crabs are definitely hiding out in there. I guess we have no option other than to leave, wait until this storm has abated, and then return and blast that cave entrance.'

'And hope that the crabs haven't moved elsewhere now that their presence has been discovered,' Cliff Davenport shook his head. Right now, though, all he wanted was to get back to Pat who would be worrying herself sick.

He knew, though, that he could not leave the Welsh coast until those crabs in the caves had been destroyed. Only then would he be able to rid himself of forty years of phobias and nightmares.

# 12

Guy N. Smith

Guy N. Smith

Downing Street had already been in contact with the Russian Embassy by the time Sanderson and Professor Danielson had changed into dry clothes and assembled with others in the latter's office. Only Cliff Davenport was absent having returned to Pat at their hotel.

Outside the storm was raging. The previous year the media had dubbed the hurricane which had swept in from the east as 'The Beast from the East', now they were calling this latest storm 'The Terror from the West'. It was reputedly the worst cyclone in the past fifty years and massive damage had resulted on the west coast of the USA with over 100 deaths recorded and many residents reported missing amidst the debris left in its wake.

Sanderson stared out of the window at the promenade in the distance, now heaped with rubble washed up from the beach below. A shelter had been demolished and parked vehicles overturned and wrecked.

'They reckon this storm is going to last for at least another couple of days,' he announced, tight lipped. 'Which means there's no chance of us blasting those crabs into oblivion until it abates.'

'Which probably will make no difference to the outcome,' Danielson replied. 'As we know that monster chasing our divers drew back when it encountered the sheer force of the waves. It and its companions are doubtless huddled in the caves awaiting the storm to abate before emerging and going in search of food. If we time it right, we can blast 'em all to hell whilst they're still in there.'

'Fingers crossed,' Sanderson pursed his lips. 'Right now, all we can do is sit and wait.'

'God, am I glad to see you back safe and sound!' Pat Davenport wrung her hands together as she watched her husband donning a dry set of clothes. 'I've been absolutely frantic. Now, please, can we go back home?'

'There's no chance of us going anywhere in this!' He indicated the rain splattered window.

At that moment a tile came off the roof. They heard it smash on the ground below. 'Just going outside would be dangerous. And I fully expect that the roads homewards will be blocked by fallen trees.'

'So we just sit it out in here,' she muttered. 'You won't be going back on the beach after the storm, though, will you?'

'I don't know right now,' he replied, dropping his gaze. 'If I do then it will only be to watch from a distance whilst those soldiers blow up that cave. At least then I'll know that the crabs are destroyed once and for all and maybe that will be the end of my phobias.'

'I suppose I'll have to go along with it,' she sighed.

Would this dammed business never end?

An emergency meeting was taking place in the Prime Minister's private office at 10 Downing Street. In attendance were the Foreign Secretary and Defence Secretary. All three had grim expressions and momentarily there was an uneasy silence.

Russian television and radio had already issued a grim statement following a telephone call to the embassy concerning the fate of the submarine which had entered UK waters.

'One of our submarines had ventured into UK waters purely on an experimental mission to test the effectiveness of new technology which had been installed. It carried no weaponry and its purpose was to discover whether or not it could be detected by patrolling ships, helicopters or drones.'

'It was detected, and an attack followed by a UK submarine causing damage which allowed water to penetrate thus drowning the crew of three. Now our submarine is held by the British and we are demanding its immediate return together with the bodies of those who died.

'This is clearly an act of war and we await an announcement from our President on what action will be taken.'

'Scientists at Porton Down are currently examining this technology,' the Defence secretary broke the uneasy silence, 'We need to know how it operates and, more importantly, how we can infiltrate its anti-detection system otherwise Russian subs will be invading our waters whenever they choose. Furthermore, it has already been proved that the attack was carried out by a large and powerful marine creature, presumably a crab or crabs. There can be no doubt about that. And as we already believe that these crustaceans are inhabiting caves in the cliffs, less than a mile from where the attack was carried out, there is no possible other explanation. The submarine was too strong for them to break into it but the damage incurred by their attack was sufficient to allow water to penetrate and drown the occupants who, incidentally, were senior GRU officers. In a nutshell, that's it!'

'As we are already aware from past instances concerning British spies murdered on our shores,' the PM stated 'the Russians will attempt to explain their innocence with the most unbelievable lies. In effect we are banging our heads against a brick wall. President Putin and his office will never accept that this was an attack by giant crustaceans, no matter how much proof we present them with. In addition to their underwater trespass it was a spying mission.'

'We can only strengthen our patrols,' the Defence Secretary stated, 'and watch and wait for any further outcome. We have never been closer to war now than we were back in the 1960's when the Cuban Crisis arose.'

The meeting broke up and the Prime Minister prepared for a meeting with a gathering of journalists who had assembled outside. They, too, would need much convincing of recent events.

13

Guy N. Smith

The full force of the storm had passed on up into the mountains, yet full strength winds and lashing rain still swept the Welsh coast two mornings later. It would probably be another twenty-four hours before anything resembling calmer weather replaced it. Nevertheless, a small group of locals had ventured out. A massive transporter carrying the damaged submarine away had attracted attention along with police and military vehicles. What the hell had been going on down there on the beach? Everybody was curious, hence a few of them braved the remnants of the Terror from the West, seeking any scant shelter from which to view the beach below the cliffs.

That was when Reuben Ryan wheeled his surfboard on a trolley from behind his parent's house, and bracing himself against the remnants of the storm, struggled towards the track that led down to the shore.

Reuben had just celebrated his twenty-third birthday,

tall and red-haired, he worked part time in the building trade, on call when he was needed. His favourite hobby was water skiing out in the bay. The past forty-eight hours had been impossible even for somebody of his fearless nature. Now, though, with the worst of the hurricane having gone inland the rough sea presented a challenge, especially as a small crowd had gathered in the shelter of a pile of rocks. He would show them what he was capable of, display his fearlessness when there was not another single bather in sight.

The incoming tide was splashing on the bottom of the cliff face. Clad only in bathing trucks he struggled with his lightweight surfing board in search of deeper water.

Staying upright was impossible as he lay full length on his lightweight craft, he attempted to paddle but it was nigh impossible. Damn it, the strong current would take him back to shore.

A glance to his rear revealed that bunch of spectators. He welcomed an audience, the opportunity to display his contempt for the conditions. If only he could paddle sideways, a hundred meters or so...

Up above, a patrolling coastguard had joined the throng, an expression of annoyance on his weather-beaten features at the sight of a water skier out there in such conditions.

'Bloody idiot!' He grunted. A rescue mission was a strong possibility. He pulled a mobile phone out from beneath the waterproof jacket.

Something bumped the underside of Reuben's

lightweight craft, lifting it above the tide, then dropping it back with a splash. An incoming wave submerged it briefly. He held on tightly, somehow preventing himself from being dislodged and deposited in the water.

Face down, through his blurred goggles he discerned a shape, a rounded sandy coloured shell from which protruded huge pincers, clawing up and attempting to reach the bobbing craft. Even through his restricted watery vision he recognised it as a giant crab!

His scream was silenced by a mouthful of saltwater. That pincer now secured a grip on the frail craft, tipped it sideways and catapulted Reuben overboard. In crazed realisation of what was happening, he instinctively attempted to swim towards the shore.

Within a couple of metres of the panic-stricken threshing of his limbs he felt something grip an ankle, closed on it and almost severed the foot. Blinding pain engulfed him; another attempted scream was stifled by an intake of salt water. His injured leg and arm flailed as he was pulled below the surface.

The crab began to drag its victim shorewards, shambling in the strong current until it emerged close to that cave opening in full view of the horrified human spectators for a few seconds before it vanished.

The small watching crowd stared in horror and disbelief at the sight which had been briefly revealed to them. Screams were whipped away in the strong wind. The coastguard phoned again, but had difficulty in speaking; producing a garbled plea for assistance from their base at Barmouth.

Neither land nor sea rescue was likely to save that water-skier, the fool had paid the ultimate price for his stupidity. If only they had been able to detonate that explosive device and seal the cave before the full strength of the Terror from the West had struck this coastline.

14

Guy N. Smith

'Well,' Sanderson stared out of the window at the rain, saw that it had eased somewhat. He glanced round at his companions, Danielson, a couple of soldiers and a coastguard. 'I guess we'll…'

At that moment his mobile phone rang. As he listened his expression became one of surprise and shock. 'Good God! We'll be right down!'

'A crab,' he addressed the others. 'It's just gone into that cave… dragging a human victim with it, some bloody fool of a surfer who risked drowning but instead fell victim to a giant crab. Well, at least we know that it's back in the caves. All we need to do now is to blow up the entrance and the devils will be buried in there forever!'

The door opened and Cliff Davenport entered. 'Something happened?' He enquired.

'Well, we can get 'em now,' Sanderson replied.

'That's providing we can make it along the shore. The worst of the storm has passed on but from what the coastguard told me the tide is still pretty rough.' He glanced questioningly at the two soldiers. 'What do you chaps think?'

'It won't be easy,' one replied, 'but we'll give it a go.'

The party filed out in silence. Right now there was nothing more to be said. Success was in the lap of the gods.

The giant crustacean shambled through the deep pool and entered the maze of caverns.

There was still a vestige of life left in its victim in spite of the water he had swallowed and the blood that poured from his foot. Reuben had given up trying to scream, now he prayed for death to come to release him from his agony and terror.

The crab halted where the channel became less deep. It hungered for food after being trapped in here throughout the storm, but it knew in its own way that it had a family to feed; youngsters which were incapable of hunting the seabed for themselves. It severed a foot, began to chew upon it, resisted the urge to rip the body to shreds.

There were other fully-grown crustaceans back in the big cave. They would descend upon its catch in a frenzy, rip it to shreds and feast upon it. Its young would be deprived of food and right now it would be impossible to go back out there and hunt for marine life. First, though, it would satisfy its own craving with a human arm. It tore the limb free from Reuben's body, and fed greedily upon it. Now it had no choice other than to drag the remnants of the corpse back to that cave where it would fight the other adults in an effort to provide some sustenance for its brood. Maternal instincts were uppermost even in females of monster crabs.

As it entered the main cave there was a stirring of huge crustaceans, shells knocking and scraping against protruding rocks, a threshing of the surface. Four adults scented food and surged towards the female. In the far corner a mass of small crabs joined the frenzied throng, clambered over the shell of a long dead adult. In here the crustaceans had both lived and died, their refuge from mankind over the passing years. Until they were ready to attack...

The female crouched to keep the others at bay, her pincers slashing at those which converged upon her, the dead and mutilated human pressed against the rock wall behind her in an effort to deny these crazed adults food.

A battle raged, the water foaming. The crabs were slashing at the female, their claws banging and scraping as she defended her recent find of human prey. The small ones bunched, frightened of the vicious fight.

Somewhere up above came a deep rumbling. Small fragments of rock cascaded from the sides of the cave, bounced off the crabs' shells and splashed into the water.

Outnumbered, the female crab was showing signs of injury, her massive shell chipped and cracked. She lifted a pincer, trying in vain to protect her small face. One of her eyes was torn away, her mouth was cut and oozing fluid. Another strike blinded her; she wielded a damaged pincer, but it was struck down.

The attacking foursome were victorious, sheer weight of numbers pushed their female companion aside. One of them grabbed the crumpled human corpse and tried to shield it from the others. A flurry of pincers found a hold, tore at it, ripping it apart. Each had a segment of Reuben Ryan's bloody flesh and bone, chewing voraciously on the still warm pieces of his corpse.

The female sank down in a heap. Watching in terror, the youngsters huddled in a corner fearful for their own fate. Another shower of rocks from above bounced off adult and infant shells. The water foamed.

From high up above the cliff rumbled and shook.

15

Guy N. Smith

Heads bowed in an attempt to shield them from the rain and wind, Sanderson's party arrived down on the beach, knee deep in the incoming tide. Up above that group of spectators were waving; their shouts whipped away by the elements.

The group crouched behind a pile of rocks which offered scant protection.

'D'you think you can make it up to the cave entrance?' Sanderson shouted through cupped hands into the ear of the solider struggling to carry the replacement explosive device.

'Dunno,' the other grimaced, 'but we'll give it a go now that we're here.' His companion nodded his agreement.

The pair set off, holding on to each other for support.

'Let's hope this is it,' Sanderson spoke everybody's

hopes aloud, 'then we can all go home.'

Cliff Davenport longed for a pipe of tobacco, but it would have been impossible in these conditions. He was tense, memories of that crustacean invasion of the coastline flooded back, almost as terrifying as they had been all those years ago. The crabs were virtually invincible, it was difficult to convince himself that this time they would be destroyed once and for all. Trapped inside the cliffs, they would surely starve to death.

Unless... a disturbing thought crept upon him. Both Adrian and Calvin had described the maze of tunnels within that cliff. Could there possibly be another exit somewhere, a passage leading away from here and so far undiscovered? No, surely not at such a popular holiday resort where visitors scoured every inch of the shoreline.

He shrugged off his doubts and fears, the purpose of his recent visit was to put his phobias to rest once and for all. Damn it, he was determined to do that at all costs.

Way up ahead the two soldiers were making slow progress. The incoming tide was stronger than they had anticipated, on one occasion a wave had washed over them but still they battled on. Another fifty yards...

Suddenly the cliff face above the cave entrance began to crack, a wide fissure that sent a number of small rocks showering down, splashing onto the shore around that underwater cave.

'Hold back!' One soldier grabbed the other. 'The cliff's starting to come apart above the cave entrance!'

Both men stared. A huge section of rock was leaning

outwards, suspended precariously.

A shower of small rocks descended from it. 'There's going to be an avalanche. Get back before it's too late!'

They turned, almost fell on the uneven surface beneath the tide, and clung desperately to each other. Behind them the large section of the cliff finally broke away, coming crashing down. A mighty splash followed as it fell into the pool below. Another fall followed it.

In desperation the two soldiers fought their way back. In the distance they saw their companions waving frantically. There was further rumbling and crashing from behind them as another huge section of rock parted company from the cliff face. It had withstood such storms from time immoral but had finally surrendered to the ravages of the pounding sea.

'Thank God you're safe,' Sanderson pulled them into their scant shelter. 'Another few minutes and you would have been buried beneath that lot.'

'Well at least we don't have to blow the cave up now.' The soldiers lowered the explosive device to the ground. 'The Terror from the West' has done it for us. Nothing will get in or out of those caves now!'

They stood watching the distant rockfall. A sizeable section of the cliff face had parted company from the main structure. Now the avalanche had ceased. Nature had decreed that her task was complete. She had trapped the crabs within their hiding place.

'Well, there's no point in stopping here,' Sanderson turned away, the others following in his wake. 'When the storm has gone, we can check that cave entrance, but I doubt that we'll be able to see it.'

Cliff Davenport breathed a huge sigh of relief. Already he sensed that those crustacean phobias which had plagued him for forty years had finally been put to rest. He prayed that they had.

16

Guy N. Smith

The following day Cliff accompanied Sanderson, Danielson, a couple of coastguards and the soldiers along to the beach past Shell Island and on towards the cliff face.

The storm had abated, gone on inland, weakening all the time. The incoming tide rippled instead of foaming, and overhead the sun shone out of a clear blue sky with only a few drifting white clouds. Summer had returned. Cliff unbuttoned his waterproof jacket; the day was warming up.

He was tense. Would they find what they hoped to discover; the cave entrance buried for all time beneath a huge fall of rocks from the cliff above? He paused to light his pipe and dropped behind the others like he was nervous about what they might see. Suppose that rock fall had missed the cave, leaving the pool and the underwater entrance open... Well, if it had then they would blow it up, he consoled himself.

Those up ahead of him had arrived at the scene. Somewhat in trepidation, Cliff joined them. They were all staring at the mighty pile of boulders that had come down from up above, stretching out to meet the incoming tide. That section of the shore was unrecognizable from their previous visits. High up above another section of the cliff had come loose and was leaning out precariously. In due course it would undoubtedly spill down into the huge fall beneath.

The pool was buried, just a small trickle of water flowing out from its extremity under the rocks.

'Well,' there was no mistaking Sanderson's triumph as he pointed to the scene. 'I guess that's it, no need to detonate a charge of explosive. Mother Nature has done the job for us and she couldn't have done it better. It's like she had finally got fed up of harbouring those crabs, hiding them from humans!'

'Yes,' Davenport let out a long sigh of relief, 'She couldn't have done a better job, better than even a charge of explosive could have done!'

The party turned away and began retracing their steps. A sense of euphoria stemmed from the sheer relief at what they had witnessed.

'I guess there's going to be an awkward situation with the Russians now,' Sanderson voiced his thoughts. 'I had a phone call from Downing Street last night. The bodies of the three members of the crew are going to be collected and they want their submarine back.

'According to what the Foreign Secretary told me it

was fitted with an electric engine which emits less heat, so our patrols were unable to detect it in UK waters. The Russians are determined to outwit our enemy defence system. I read in the paper recently that we are developing an airplane with 'Star Wars' technology; laser weapons capable of shooting down enemy planes. This means that these planes would not run out of ammunition providing their engines could generate enough power. Around nine are ready to be deployed on operation. The paper also said that the existing Typhoons have been supplied with new missiles to boost their firepower. They claim that Britain now has the capability to defend itself. All in all, though, it is a worrying situation.'

'Well, at least the crabs are out of the way,' Danielson stated. 'But in their place, we've got these giant jellyfish in our waters. They could well be out next marine problem. They are as dangerous as the giant crabs!'

'Well?' Pat Davenport had waited anxiously in the hotel's foyer for her husband's return.

'They're gone for good,' he replied, 'trapped in their cliff hideaway by one of the largest rockfalls I've ever seen.'

'Thank God!' There was no mistaking her relief. 'Can we finally go home now?'

'Indeed, we can,' he laughed, 'but I think we'll have a celebration meal before we leave. I have a feeling that, like the giant crustaceans, my phobias are dead and buried!'

They embraced in undisguised ecstasy and sheer relief.

# ABOUT THE AUTHOR

Guy N. Smith has been a best-selling author for over 40 years. He has published 120 novels and around 400 short stories and articles on various subjects.

*Night of the Crabs* became an instant best seller with the movie rights sold. Since then there have been no fewer than 7 sequels. *Killer Crabs* is currently being filmed.

Find out more at www.guynsmith.com

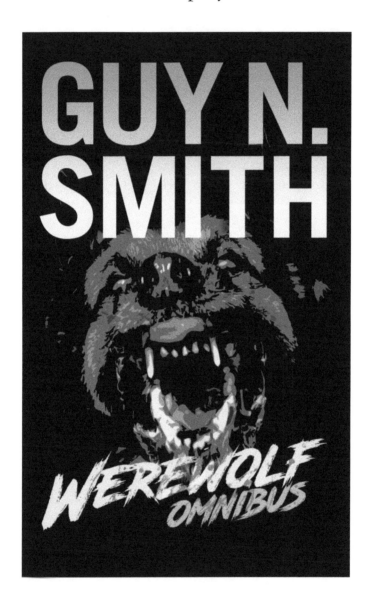

# Guy N. Smith's
# Werewolf Omnibus

Are werewolves simply folklore or have they existed at some stage in the distant past?

Lycanthropy is known to be a mental condition where the sufferer believes himself to be a wolf and embarks upon a psychotic rampage. So perhaps there's some truth in the age-old legends.

The Black Hill in South Shropshire is a dark forest where legend becomes reality. As well as werewolves seeking human prey, the hills hold tales of the black dogs. A sighting of these spectral canines is a harbinger of death.

Gordon Hall, the sporting tenant, finds himself caught up in these ancient horrors and is determined to destroy them once and for all.

Both his life and his soul are at risk.

Werewolf Omnibus collects together three vintage novels from the master of pulp horror, Guy N. Smith: Werewolf By Moonlight (1974), Return Of The Werewolf (1977) and The Son Of The Werewolf (1978), alongside a new short story, Spawn Of The Werewolf.

# The Black Room Manuscripts Volume Three

Guy N. Smith features in *The Black Room Manuscripts Volume Three* with his short story **Toad In The Hole**.

All profits made the sale of this book go to the charity Shelter.

# The Black Room Manuscripts Volume Three

SINISTER
HORROR
COMPANY

Some words are born in shadows.

Some tales told only in whispers.

Under the paper thin veneer of our sanity is a world that exists. Hidden just beyond, in plain sight, waiting to consume you should you dare stray from the street-lit paths that sedate our fears.

For centuries the Black Room has stored stories of these encounters, suppressing the knowledge of the rarely seen. Protecting the civilised world from its own dark realities.

The door to the Black Room has once again swung open to unleash twenty five masterful tales of the macabre from the twisted minds of a new breed of horror author.

The Black Room holds many secrets.

Dare you enter...for a third time?

# Guy N. Smith Illustrated Bibliography

"The sheer effort and dedication that's gone into creating this unbelievably comprehensive bibliography is breath-taking." – DLS Reviews

The complete(ish) guide to collecting the works of Guy N. Smith.

A journey into collecting the works of prolific author Guy Newman Smith. The book covers all genres of the Great Scribbler's writing and contains over 950 pictures and useful details to assist any would-be collector.

# Guy N. Smith Illustrated Bibliography

The author has endeavoured to list and visually represent, through over 950 colour pictures, the vast catalogue of output from Guy N. Smith's 65+ years in print; from the early stories he had published in the Tettenhall Observer and Advertiser paper as a teenager through to the present day. A career that crosses fiction and non-fiction and has covered almost all possible genres along the way, from Self-Sufficiency to Westerns, via Countryside and Glamour magazines of the 70s, all in addition to the numerous horror and thriller titles he is better known for.

Content includes Fiction (all imprints/editions inc. non UK) and Non-Fiction Categories: Horror, Thriller, Countryside and Children's Novels, Omnibus Collections, Chapbooks, Graphic Novels, Anthologies, Fanzines, Booklets, Magazines (70s adult Glamour, Country Sport, Game-keeping, Horror etc.), Periodicals and Newspapers.

The book also contains an original Guy N. Smith short story 'The Beast in the Cage' along with humorous insight into the levels of collecting Guy N. Smith's works in 'The Completist- A Cautionary Tale' by author Shane P.D Agnew.

A4 Size, 950+ colour pictures, 341 pages.

Available via Amazon.

The Sinister Horror Company is an independent UK
publisher of genre fiction. Their mission a simple one –
to write, publish and launch innovative and exciting
genre fiction by themselves and others.

For further information on the Sinister Horror
Company visit:

SinisterHorrorCompany.com
Facebook.com/sinisterhorrorcompany
Twitter @SinisterHC

SINISTERHORRORCOMPANY.COM

Lightning Source UK Ltd.
Milton Keynes UK
UKHW040153180221
378934UK00002B/292